Basil the Bear Cub

by Janey Louise Jones

illustrated by Jennie Poh

PICTURE WINDOW BOOKS
a capstone imprint

Superfairies is published by Picture Window Books
A Capstone Imprint
1710 Roe Crest Drive
North Mankato, Minnesota 56003
www.mycapstone.com

Library of Congress Cataloging-in-Publication Data

Names: Jones, Janey, 1968- author. | Poh, Jennie,
illustrator.
Title: Basil the bear cub / by Janey Louise Jones ;
illustrated by Jennie Poh.
Description: North Mankato, Minnesota : Picture
Window Books, 2016. | Series: Superfairies | Summary:
When Basil the bear cub falls into the river, it is up to the
superfairies to rescue him before he gets swept over the
waterfall.
Identifiers: LCCN 2015037868| ISBN 9781479586417
(library binding) | ISBN 9781479586455 (pbk.) | ISBN
9781479586493 (ebook pdf)
Subjects: LCSH: Bear cubs--Juvenile fiction. | Fairies-
-Juvenile fiction.   Rescues--Juvenile fiction. | CYAC:
Bears--Fiction. | Fairies--Fiction.   Rescues--Fiction.
Classification: LCC PZ7.J72019 Bas 2016 | DDC [E]--
dc23
LC record available at http://lccn.loc.gov/2015037868

Designer: Alison Thiele

For my husband Jake, and our two little fairies
Aurelia and Evangeline x — Jennie Poh

Printed and bound in US.
007522CGS16

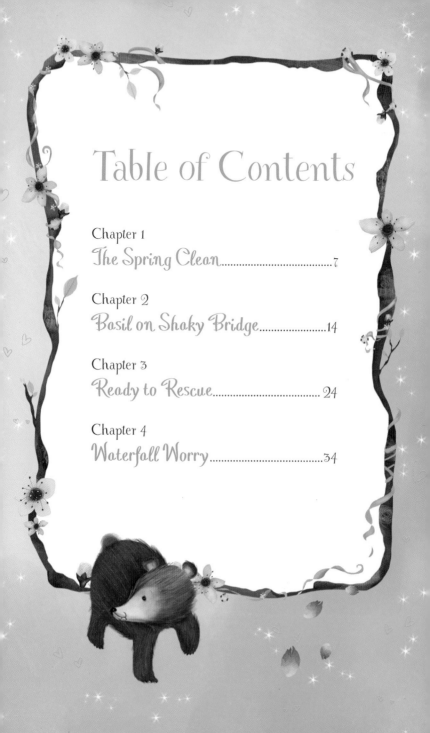

Table of Contents

The Fairy World

The Superfairies of Peaseblossom Woods use teamwork to rescue animals in trouble. They bring together their special superskills, petal power and lots of love.

Superfairy Rose

can blow super healing fairy kisses to make the animals in Peaseblossom Woods feel better.

Superfairy Berry
can see for miles
around with her
super eyesight.

Superfairy Star
can create super dazzling
brightness in one dainty spin
to lighten up dark places.

Superfairy Silk
spins super strong webs
for animal rescues.

Chapter 1

The Spring Clean

The cold wind and snow of winter passed over Peaseblossom Woods and the warm spring sun shone brightly over the trees.

Flowers bloomed.

Birds sang.

Bumblebees buzzed.

While the Superfairies were busy preparing for an exciting new season of animal rescues, all the animals of Peaseblossom Woods were slowly waking up from a long, cozy winter sleep …

"Yawn!" snuffled Susie Squirrel.

"Gosh, I'm so hungry!" squeaked Mrs. Mouse.

"Oh! What a lovely long sleep that was!" mumbled Mr. Badger.

"Splish-splash!" went Toby Otter as he flopped into the river.

"I'd like to explore!" said Basil Bear, rubbing his bleary eyes.

The Superfairies were spring cleaning their home inside the cherry blossom tree.

Rose was in charge of organizing their closet. She sang cheerfully as she washed all their pretty spring petal dresses, and arranged their ribbons and dainty shoes.

"Roses and lilies, violets too. Blossom so pink and bluebells so blue. Doo-be-doo-be-doo, flowers so true."

From time to time, she dreamed up some new dress designs, which she immediately doodled on her Strawberry computer.

"I'll show these sketches to the others later," she decided.

Meanwhile, Silk was dancing as she cleaned the bedroom and dusted the furniture with a feather duster ...

twirl

hop

skip

spin
and repeat

She could hear Rose's song and soon joined in:

"Blossom so pink and bluebells so blue ..."

Over in the storeroom, Berry was sorting through the supplies of honey, herbs, fruits, vegetables, and berries left over from the cold winter months.

She wrote labels for the jars and boxes:

Peaseblossom Healing Honey
Bumblicious!

Fresh Herbs
Peppermint. Parsley. Sage

Scrumptious Sweet Fruit
Tutti Frutti-tastic

Super Berries
Super Juicy, Super Yummy

Various Vegetables for
Soups, Stews, Juice, and Dips

Berry began to hum along to the song as well …

"Doo-be-doo-be-doo, flowers so true …"

Meanwhile, Star was carefully counting and washing their collection of sparkling gemstones in a basin of spring water, lavender, and lemon juice. Sometimes they used the gems to help with their rescues.

"One moonstone. Twinkly.

Two rose quartz stones. Sparkly.

Three amber stones. Gleaming.

Four ruby stones. Dazzling.

Five sapphire stones. Stunning ..." she said to herself.

Then she caught a bar of the song, and joined in. *"Roses and lilies, violets too ..."*

And the harder the Superfairies worked, the sweeter their song sounded. They loved to work as a team.

Chapter 2

Basil on Shaky Bridge

The sun grew warmer, and the day became brighter.

Down at the riverbank, Basil Bear Cub wandered along in search of a playmate.

He threw twigs into the water as he went.

"It's fun to be away from Mom and Dad!" he said. "But I'm a little bored on my own."

One of the twigs he threw made a huge splash!

The water splashed right over Toby Otter, who was lying on a big stone enjoying the warmth of the sun.

"Hey! What made that splash?" he cried, looking up to the riverbank.

"Oops, sorry — that was me!" called Basil. "I threw a stick. I didn't see you there."

Toby Otter sat up. "It's okay," he said. "Getting wet is what I do. Do you want to play?"

"Yes, please!" said Basil. "I'd love to!"

"Come down to the water," said the little otter.

Basil edged forward nervously.

"Come all the way down," said Toby Otter. "It's fun down here."

Back at the cherry blossom tree, the Superfairies had almost finished their cleaning work.

"It won't be long now until the animals wake from their winter sleep," said Rose, as she hung up the last petal dress to dry. "It will be lovely to see them all again."

The Superfairies sat down to a delicious lunch together in their kitchen.

Berry brought a salad bowl from the storeroom, brimming with herbs, fruits, crunchy vegetables, and berries. Rose appeared with fresh lavender bread, which had come from the Badger's Bakehouse, spread with fresh butter from Fairydell Farm. All of this was washed down with minted peach-water.

"I can't wait to see our furry friends," said Rose.

"Me too!" chorused the other fairies.

"And there will be lots of new babies!" said Berry. "I love the babies!"

"Let's have some honeycomb and vanilla cake to celebrate spring," suggested Silk. She took a beautiful big cake tin down from the top shelf.

Then:

Ting-aling-aling …

There was a faint ringing sound in the distance.

"Does that sound like the rescue bells ringing?" said Berry.

"It does! It is!" said Silk. "One of the animals in the woods must be in trouble!"

Ting-aling-aling …

Ting-aling-aling …

The ringing got much louder.

"Oh dear! We must get our wands as quickly as possible!" said Star.

"I'll check the fairycopter for fuel!" said Berry. "We'll definitely need the fairycopter if an animal has to be air-lifted to safety."

"Yes, and I'll grab our Strawberry computer!" called Rose.

"Let me fill the fairy rescue pack," said Silk.

In a twinkle-spin-flutter, the Superfairies were ready to rescue. They sat in their fairycopter, ready for take-off. Berry was at the controls as usual, because her super eyesight enabled her to see any problems ahead.

Rose checked the Strawberry computer to see where the problem was.

"Oh look!" she said. "The screen on the Strawberry is showing a picture of Shaky Bridge — that's such a dark, dangerous spot!"

"Let's get going," said Berry. "Are we ready for take-off?"

"I'll read through the checklist of what should be in our fairy rescue pack," said Star. "Let me know if you've packed everything, Silk."

☑ Extra Wings
☑ Warming Feather Cloak
☑ Peaseblossom Healing Honey
☑ Energizing Fruit Smoothie
☑ Healing Gemstones
☑ Olive Oil

"Nothing missing," confirmed Silk. "Ready for take-off now."

"5, 4, 3, 2, 1 ... go, go, go!" said Rose.

With the help of a passing gust of wind, Berry flew the fairycopter up, up, up over Peaseblossom Woods. Soon they were soaring in the sky. They followed the line of the river, swooping past Lavender Lane and the Strawberry Fields.

"It looks very dark up ahead at Shaky Bridge," said Berry, using her super eyesight. "Star, we will need all the brightness we can get. Please prepare to dazzle!"

"Ready to dazzle at any time!" said Star.

Chapter 3

Ready to Rescue

As they approached the part of the river where Shaky Bridge spanned the water, all the fairies except Berry flew out of the fairycopter.

Berry brought the fairycopter down, down, down … softly, gently, carefully … and landed it safely in a woodland clearing. Then she flew to join the others.

It was a very dark and gloomy part of the woods. The branches of the trees hung heavily over the river, and the wobbly old bridge cast looming shadows over the water.

Twinkle!

Dazzle!

Sparkle!

Tada!

"I will soon lighten this place up," said Star, using her powers of brightness. She began to spin.

The woods suddenly became bright.

"Thank you, Star," said Berry. "That's better. I can see clearly now."

"I can see Mother Bear by the bridge," said Berry, looking ahead. "She looks worried."

All the Superfairies followed Berry, and with their wands outstretched before them, they flew to where Mother Bear stood.

"Oh, thank you for coming," sobbed Mother Bear. "It's my new little cub, Basil. He wandered off and started playing with Toby Otter … and now he's dangling off Shaky Bridge! I think his paw is trapped!"

"Don't worry, Mother Bear," said Silk gently. "We will free him, you'll see!"

Toby Otter watched sadly from the edge of the water.

"I'm very sorry. I dared him to cross the bridge. It's all my fault!" he said. "I feel terrible."

"Well, I'm sure you won't do that again," said Rose. "You did the right thing by ringing the bell, Toby Otter!"

Father Bear stood in the water, talking up to his young son, who was hanging dangerously from the high bridge above.

"The Superfairies have arrived, Basil. Just do as they say, son," he said.

"Daddy, my paw hurts and I'm very hungry!" said Basil.

Poor little Basil! He was so scared.

Rose flew in close to see what they could do.

"Hello, Basil," she said, blowing him a soothing fairy kiss. "Let me see what is trapping your paw."

"Your kiss has made my paw feel better," said Basil. "But it's still stuck."

The Superfairies fluttered around him, thinking about the best way to free him.

"A piece of wood is stuck across his paw. We need to remove it. Then he will be able to move," said Silk. The fairies worked very hard to move the piece of wood.

Star and Silk swished their wands over it, hoping it might give a little, while Rose and Berry tried to move the plank of wood. But it was stuck firmly.

"I know what to do!" said Berry. "Let's pour olive oil over Basil's paw. Then we can slide it out from under the piece of wood!"

"Good thinking!" said Rose. "Take some oil from my backpack."

As soon as the oil was poured, Basil began to wiggle his toes to free his paw.

Wiggle. Wiggle. Wiggle.

Slip. Slide. Slither.

"My paw is moving. It's free!" he cried happily.

But it worked so quickly that Basil fell

into the river below!

Splash!

"Catch him, Father Bear!" cried Mother Bear.

Father Bear *tried* to catch him. Really he did. But Basil was carried along with the flow of the river.

"Help!" cried Basil. "I can't swim yet!"

"Superfairies! Please help. Quickly!" cried Mother Bear.

Basil ducked under the water. Toby Otter started to swim next to him, saying, "You can do it!"

Basil's eyes and ears were full of water, so he couldn't hear what Toby Otter was saying.

"I can't see!" he cried. "And I can't hear!"

And still the river's current pulled him along.

Chapter 4

Waterfall Worry

The fairies flew as fast as they could, following Basil, but after a group of rocks, the river was flowing in rushing circles of fierce water.

Basil was whirled and twirled around as if he was spinning inside a washing machine!

Whoosh! He went to the left.

Then whoosh! He went to the right!

Toby Otter couldn't fight the current either. He scrambled to safety at the water's edge, watching the rescue anxiously. "I wish I could do more to help!" he said.

"Berry, get the fairycopter!" said Rose. "And Star, take our speed wings out of the pack. Oh, and Silk, go with Berry and prepare a web ladder to throw down to Basil. Focus, everyone!"

The Superfairies stepped up their rescue operation, with Rose and Star hovering over Basil. It was impossible to reach him, as he was whipping around in the jets of bubbling water.

A strong current of water lifted Basil up and propelled him with a b|ast! back out into the fast-flowing open river.

Rose and Star followed him along the river, wearing their fastest wings.

Past Badger's Drift. Past Squirrel Square. Past Lavender Lane.

"Oh no!" said Star. "Look! Basil is almost to the waterfall!"

"We *have* to save him!" said Rose.

"Basil!" called Star.

But Basil couldn't hear them because of the noise of the rushing water.

Berry and Silk flew overhead in the fairycopter and threw a web ladder down to Basil.

He didn't see it.

The waterfalls loomed up ahead.
Rose knew it wouldn't be long before
the little bear would be carried over the
edge of the rugged rocks and thrown
downwards, where the water poured like
a faucet turned on full blast.

"Please do something!" said Mother Bear. "He will never survive the falls!"

Rose spotted the Duck Family nestling into the riverbank.

"Mr. Duck!" called Rose. "Can you paddle to Basil, please, and tell him there's a ladder coming his way!

"I'll do my best!" cried Mr. Duck.

Mr. Duck used all his strength to half-paddle, half-fly out toward Basil.

He got up close to him.

"Basil!" he cried. "Look up! The fairies will throw a ladder down to you!"

The poor little bear was exhausted, but with the last bit of energy in his body, he did as Mr. Duck said and looked up.

The ladder was dangling just above him.

At first, Basil didn't catch the ladder.
He tried again …

But it slipped through his tiny paws.

"You can do it, Basil!" called his father from the riverbank. "You're strong enough. I know you are! I believe in you! Try again!"

"Your daddy says you can do it!" said Mr. Duck. "Try again, Basil! You must!"

The brave little bear cub reached out for the ladder again. He used all his strength and this time he grabbed it!

"Hooray! Don't let go, Basil," called Rose. "Good job! We're so proud of you!"

Basil was shivering and shaking and shuddering. The fairies flew around him and helped him to climb the web ladder, one rung at a time. He wobbled and swayed and sobbed.

"Another rung, Basil! You'll soon be at the fairycopter," said Star, "and we have some delicious snacks and juice in there!"

One rung at a time, he bravely wobbled his way to the top of the ladder.

At last, he was safely inside the fairycopter. Berry gave a thumbs up to Mother and Father Bear below.

"Meet us back at the cherry blossom tree!" she called.

Mother and Father Bear set off as fast as their legs would take them.

"Bravo Basil!" said Rose. "You made it, little one!"

Basil's teeth chattered so much, he couldn't speak.

"Let's wrap him in the feather cloak," said Star.

Basil snuggled thankfully into the cozy cloak.

"I'm so, so, so, *so* hungry," he said, in a croaky voice.

"How about some honey?" said Rose.

She offered him a spoonful of
Peaseblossom healing honey.

He licked the spoon. "I've never had
honey before," said Basil. "But I think I'm
going to like it!"

The fairies laughed and gave him some more, along with a tutti-frutti smoothie.

Berry landed the fairycopter back at the cherry blossom tree.

Mother and Father Bear were waiting.

Father Bear reached into the fairycopter and took Basil in his arms.

"Thank you, Superfairies!" said Father Bear. "What would we do without you?"

The fairies smiled proudly.

It was time for everyone to go inside the cherry blossom tree for some fairy fun!

The Bear family ate fairy cupcakes with the Superfairies and chatted until dark.

"From now on," said Basil, "I will never wander off without Mom and Dad again!"

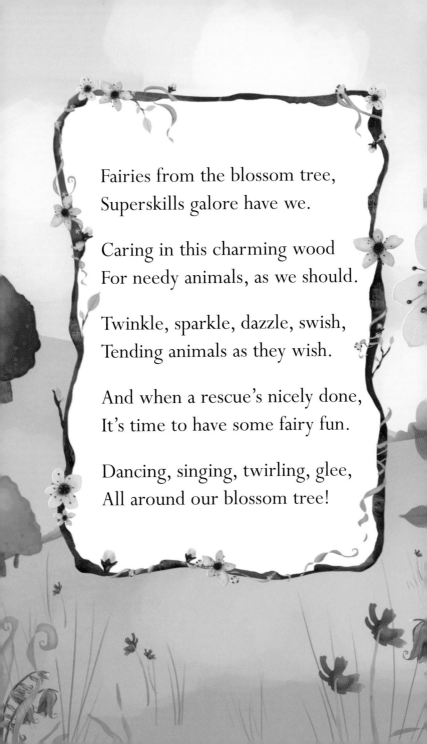

Fairies from the blossom tree,
Superskills galore have we.

Caring in this charming wood
For needy animals, as we should.

Twinkle, sparkle, dazzle, swish,
Tending animals as they wish.

And when a rescue's nicely done,
It's time to have some fairy fun.

Dancing, singing, twirling, glee,
All around our blossom tree!

Glossary

cozy (KOH-zee)—a feeling of warmth

dazzling (DAZ-ling)—extremely bright

gemstone (JEM-stohn)—a precious jewel

healing (HEEL-ing)—making someone feel
better

honey (HUHN-ee)—a sweet food made by
bees

lavender (LAV-uhn-dur)—a perfumed,
healing plant

organize (OR-guh-nize)—put in order

rescue (RESS-kyoo)—save or prevent injury

Talk It Out

1. Imagine how it would feel to be asleep all winter, then wake up to the beauty of spring. What things would be different from when you fell asleep?

2. Was it a bad idea for Basil the Bear Cub to go off without grown-ups?

3. What do you think Basil was thinking about while he was in the water?

4. Do you think Basil learned a lesson? Why or why not?

Write It Down

1. Draw a new Superfairy and give him or her a name. Write a description of his or her superskill.

2. What does the Strawberry computer tell the fairies?

3. Which superskill would you want to have? Why?

All About Fairies

The legend of fairies is as old as time. Fairy tales tell stories of fairy magic. According to legend, fairies are so small and delicate, and fly so fast, that they might actually be all around us, but just very hard to see. Fairies, supposedly, only reveal themselves to believers.

Fairies often dance in circles at sunrise and sunset. They love to play in woodlands among wildflowers. If you sing gently to them, they may appear.

Here are some of the world's most famous fairies:

The Flower Fairies

Artist Cicely Mary Barker painted a range of pretty flower fairies and published eight volumes of flower fairy art from 1923. The link between fairies and flowers is very strong.

The Tooth Fairy

She visits us during the night to leave a coin when we lose our baby teeth. Although it is very hard to catch sight of her, children are always happy when she visits.

Fake Fairies

In 1917, cousins Elsie Wright and Frances Griffiths said they photographed fairies in their garden. They later admitted that most were fakes — but Frances claimed that one was genuine.

Which Superfairy Are You?

1. If you had an allowance, would you …
   A) save it up for an adventure
   B) buy jewelry
   C) buy books
   D) buy hair clips and accessories

2. When a friend is sad, do you …
   A) take her out for an ice cream
   B) listen to the problem
   C) do a favor to make life easier for her
   D) play music and dance

3. If asked to clean your room, would you start by …
   A) putting away the clothes and shoes
   B) putting away the jewellery and bags
   C) putting away the books
   D) putting away the dress up stuff

4. Do you like perfumes that smell like …
   A) lavender
   B) rose petals
   C) fruits
   D) honeysuckle

5. If your grandma wasn't feeling well, would you …
   A) talk to her about when she was young
   B) give her flowers
   C) bake a strawberry cream cake
   D) perform a dance routine for her

6. Which herb or spice smells nicest?
   A) lavender
   B) cinnamon
   C) nutmeg
   D) mint

7. What is the best way to travel?
   A) airplane
   B) bicycle
   C) helicopter
   D) train

8. Which insect do you like most?
   A) silkworm
   B) butterfly
   C) ladybug
   D) bumblebee

Mostly A—you are like Silk. Adventurous and brave, you always think of ways to deal with problems! You enjoy action and adventures.

Mostly B—you are like Rose: gentle, kind and loving. You are good at staying calm and love pink things.

Mostly C—you are like Berry: fun, always helpful, with lots of great ideas. You are sensible and wise.

Mostly D—you are like Star. You cheer people up and dazzle with your sparkling ways! You are funny and enjoy jokes and dancing.

About the Author

Janey Louise Jones has been a published author for 10 years. Her Princess Poppy series is an international bestselling brand, with books translated into 10 languages, including Hebrew and Mandarin. Janey is a graduate of Edinburgh University and lives in Edinburgh, Scotland with her three sons. She loves fairies, princesses, beaches, and woodlands.

About the Illustrator

Jennie Poh was born in England and grew up in Malaysia (in the jungle). At the age of 10 she moved back to England and trained as a ballet dancer. She studied fine art at Surrey Institute of Art & Design as well as fashion illustration at Central Saint Martins. Jennie loves the countryside, animals, tea, and reading. She lives in Woking, England with her husband and two wonderful daughters.

JOIN THE

Superfairies

ON MORE
MAGICAL
ANIMAL RESCUES!

Basil the Bear Cub
by Janey Louise Jones

Dancer the Wild Pony
by Janey Louise Jones

Martha the Little Mouse
by Janey Louise Jones

Violet the Velvet Rabbit
by Janey Louise Jones

THE *Fun* DOESN'T STOP HERE!

For MORE GREAT BOOKS go to
WWW.MYCAPSTONE.COM